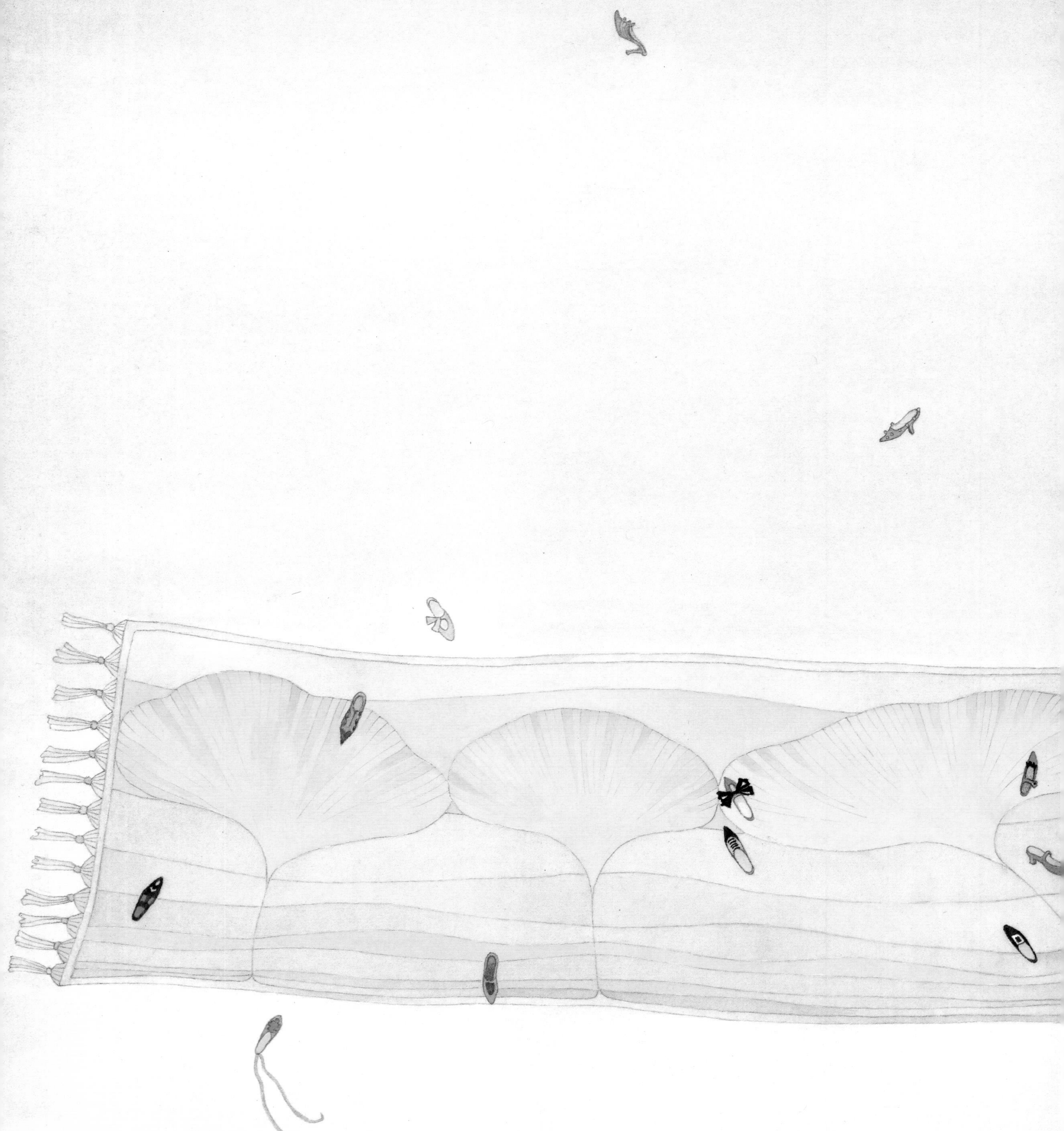

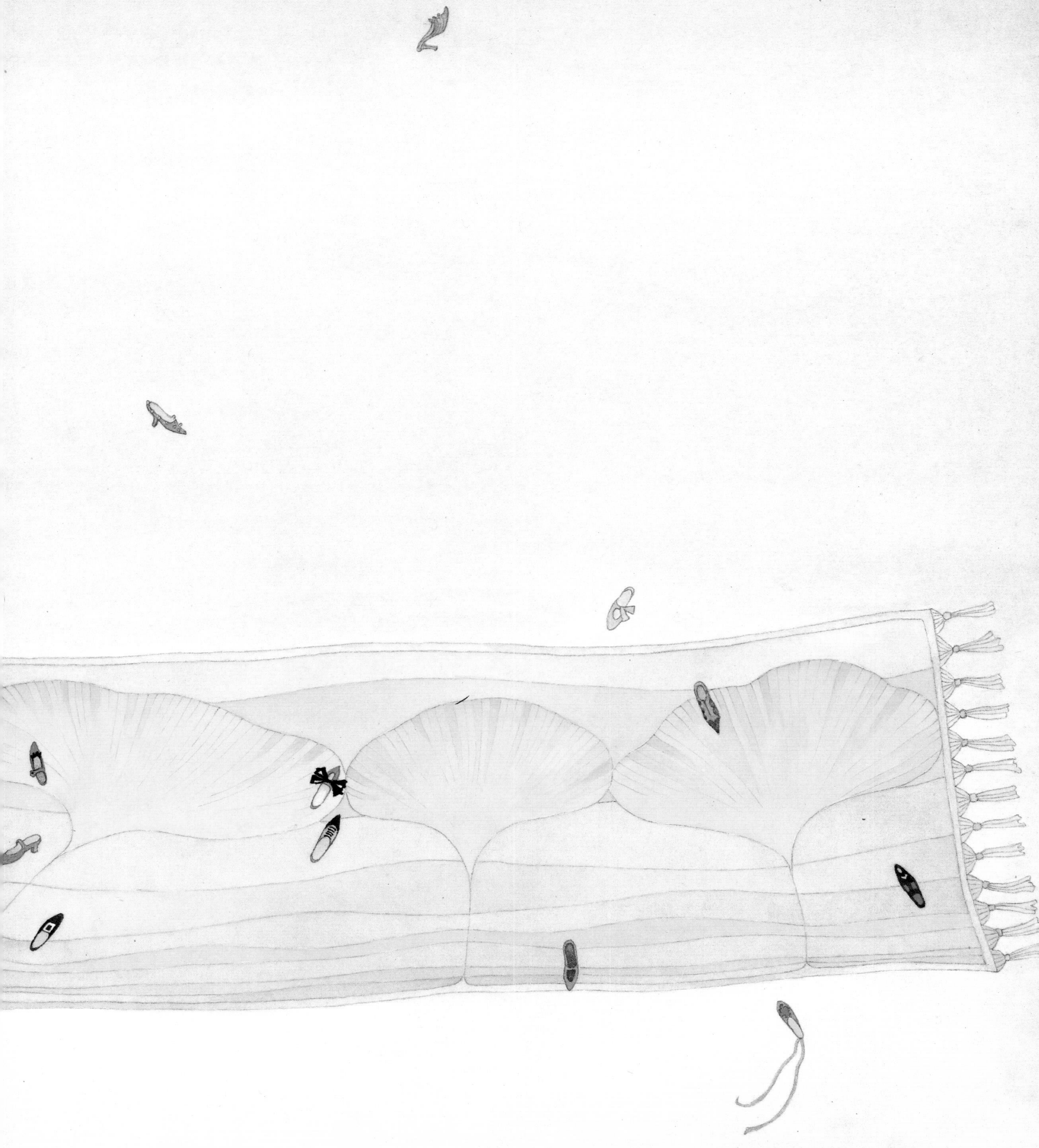

Copyright © 1995 by Nord-Süd Verlag AG, Gossau Zürich, Switzerland
First published in Switzerland under the title *Die zertanzten Schuhe*
English translation copyright © 1995 by North-South Books Inc.

First published in the United States, Great Britain, Canada, Australia,
and New Zealand in 1995 by North-South Books, an imprint of
Nord-Süd Verlag AG, Gossau Zürich, Switzerland.

Distributed in the United States by North-South Books Inc., New York.

Library of Congress Cataloging-in-Publication Data
Grimm, Jacob (1785-1863).
[Zertanzten Schuhe. English]
The twelve dancing princesses / a fairy tale by Jacob and Wilhelm Grimm;
translated from the German by Anthea Bell; illustrated by Dorothée Duntze.
Summary: To win a bride and a kingdom, a soldier endeavors to discover why the
dancing shoes of the king's twelve daughters are worn to pieces every morning.
[1. Fairy tales.   2. Folklore—Germany.]   I. Grimm, Wilhelm, 1786-1859.
II. Bell, Anthea.   III. Duntze, Dorothée, ill.   IV. Title.
PZ8.G882Tw   1995
398.2'0943'02—dc20   95-2267

A CIP catalogue record for this book is available from The British Library.

ISBN 1-55858-216-9 (trade binding) 10 9 8 7 6 5 4 3 2 1
ISBN 1-55858-217-7 (library binding) 10 9 8 7 6 5 4 3 2 1
Printed in Belgium

The Twelve Dancing Princesses

A Fairy Tale by Jacob and Wilhelm Grimm
Translated from the German by Anthea Bell

Illustrated by Dorothée Duntze

North-South Books
NEW YORK / LONDON

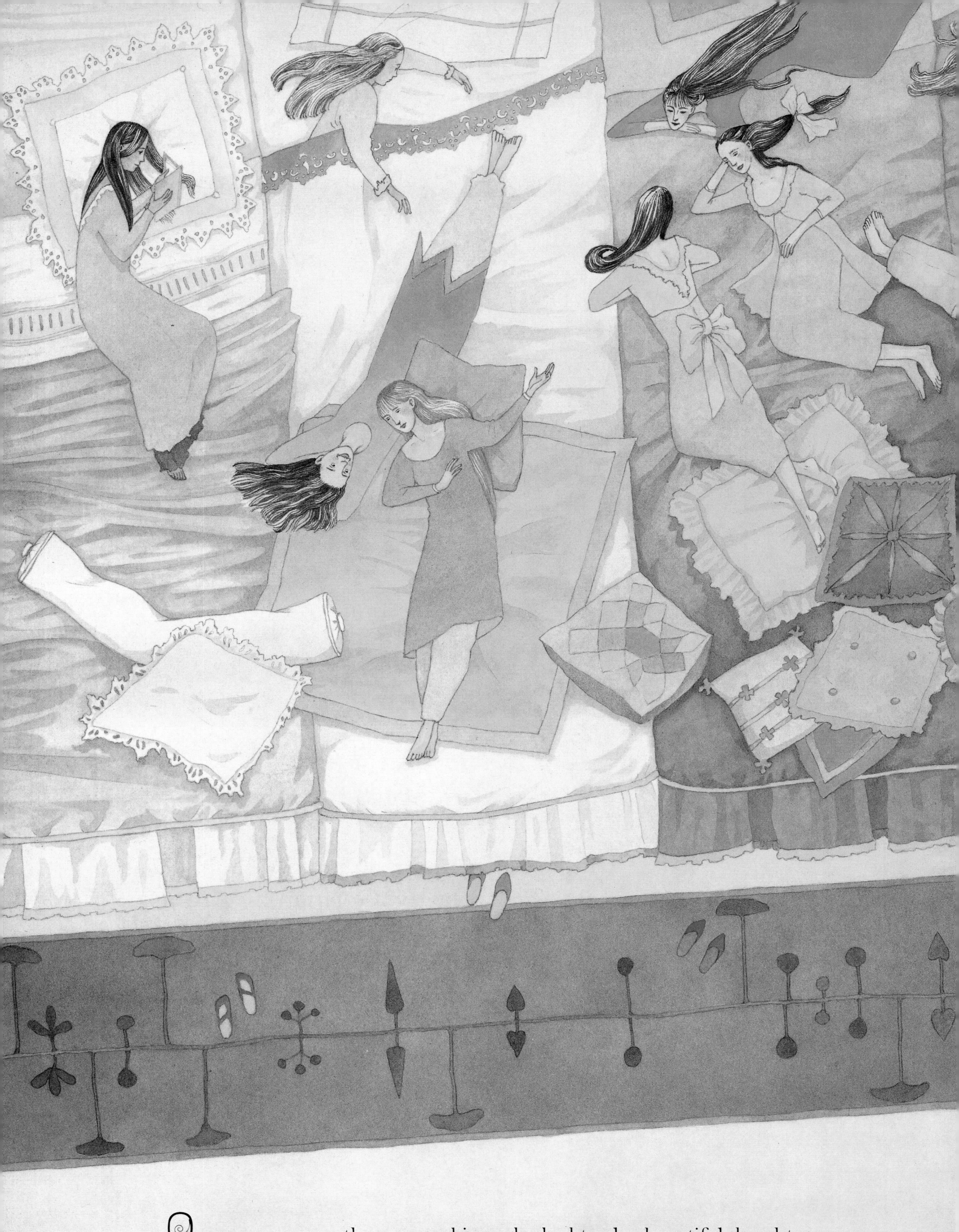

Once upon a time there was a king who had twelve beautiful daughters.

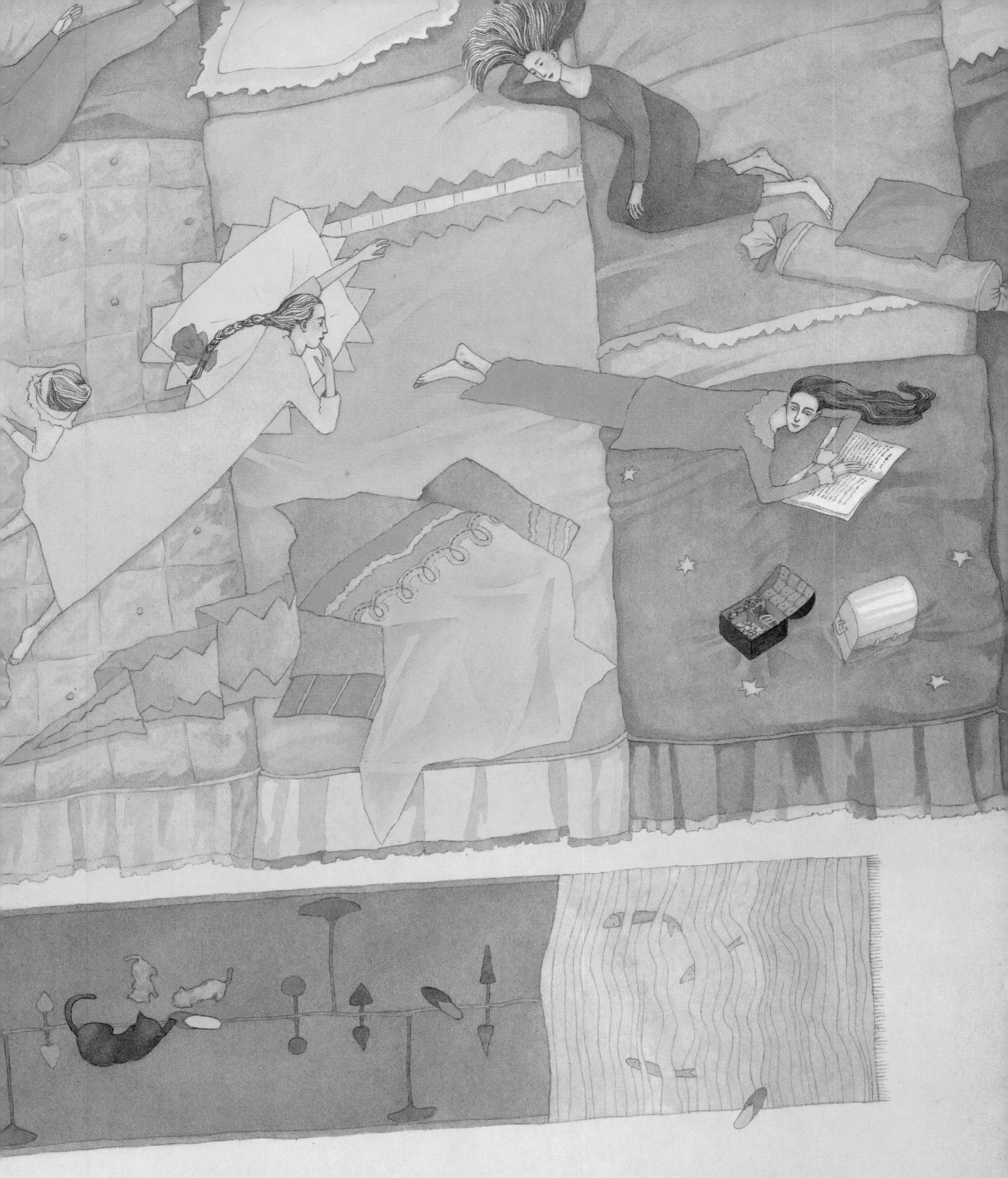

They all slept together, their beds standing side by side in a great room. Every evening, once they had gone to bed, the king closed and bolted the bedroom door. And every morning when he opened it again, he found holes in their shoes. How it happened remained a mystery.

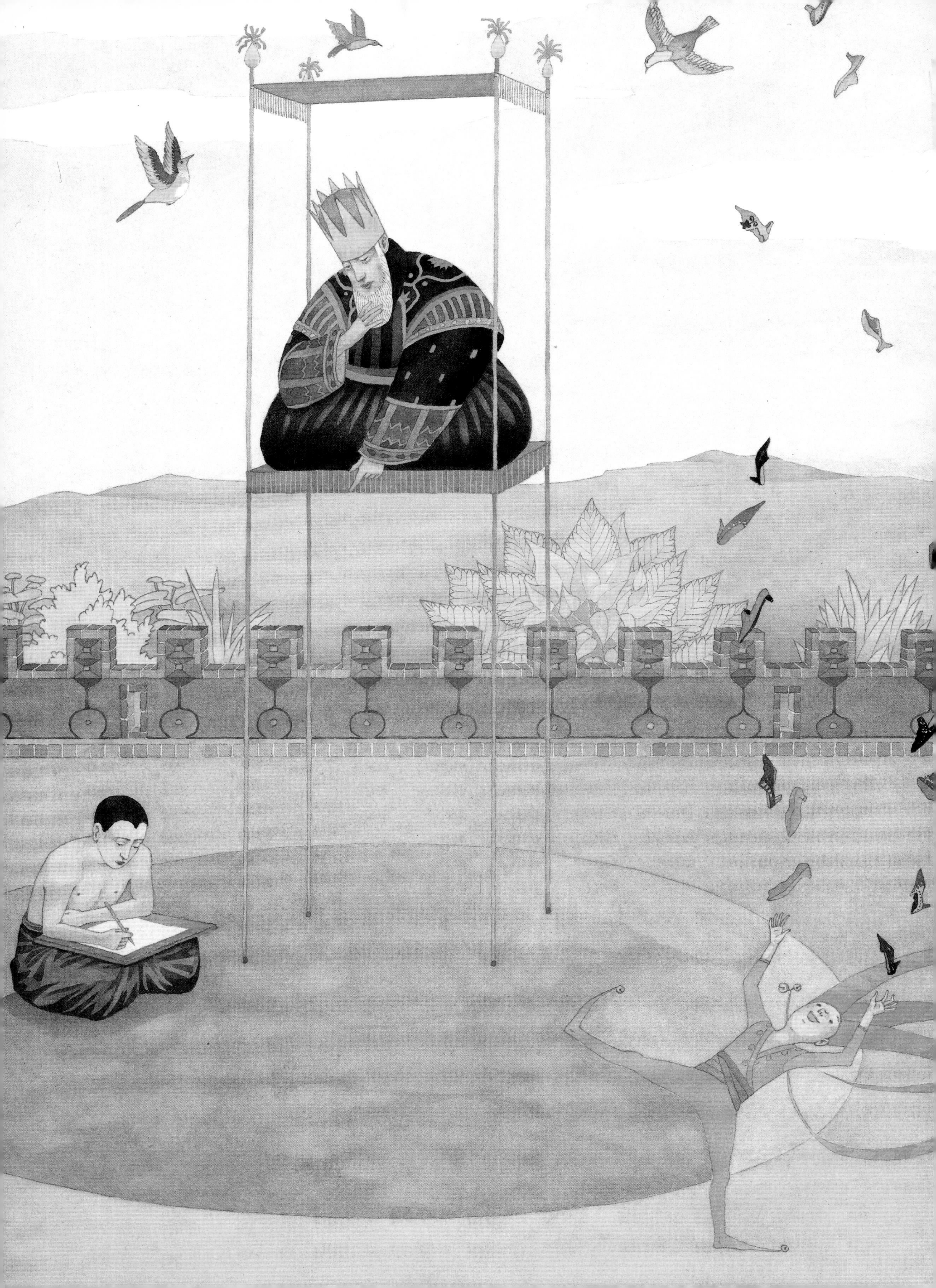

One day the king proclaimed that any man who discovered how the princesses wore out their shoes each night could choose one of them for his wife, and rule the country after the king's death. However, if he failed to solve the mystery after three days and three nights, he would be executed.

Before long, a king's son came to try his luck. He was made welcome, and in the evening he was given a room next to the great bedroom where the princesses slept. A bed had been made ready for him, but he was to keep watch and find out where the princesses went. The door to their bedroom was left open, so that they could not do anything in secret or leave by any other way.

However, the eyes of the king's son felt as heavy as lead. He fell asleep, and when he woke in the morning, the twelve princesses' shoes were in holes again. The same thing happened on the second evening, and the third evening too, so the prince's head was cut off without mercy.

Many others came after him, hoping to solve the riddle, but they all lost their lives as well.

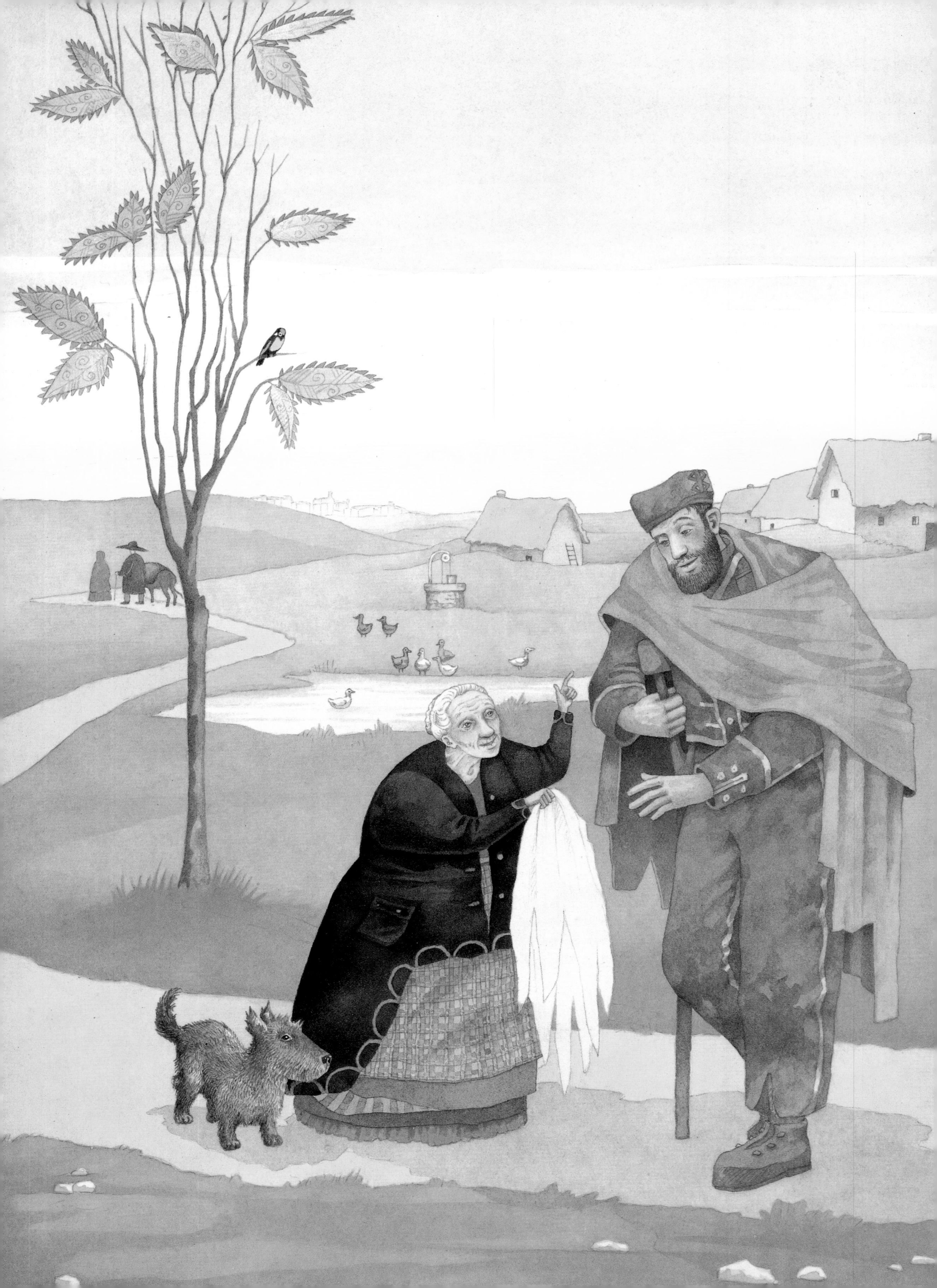

One day a poor soldier who had been wounded in battle met an old woman on the road, and she asked where he was going.

"I hardly know!" he said, and he added, for a joke, "Though I wouldn't mind finding out how the king's daughters wear holes in their shoes and become king myself one day!"

"That's not so difficult as you may think," said the old woman. "Just don't drink the wine they bring you in the evening, and pretend to be fast asleep." Then she gave him a cape and said, "If you put this cape on, you'll be invisible, and you can follow the twelve princesses unseen."

The soldier took this good advice seriously. Plucking up his courage, he went to see the king and said he had come to seek the hand of one of the princesses in marriage. He was welcomed as hospitably as their other suitors and given royal clothes to wear.

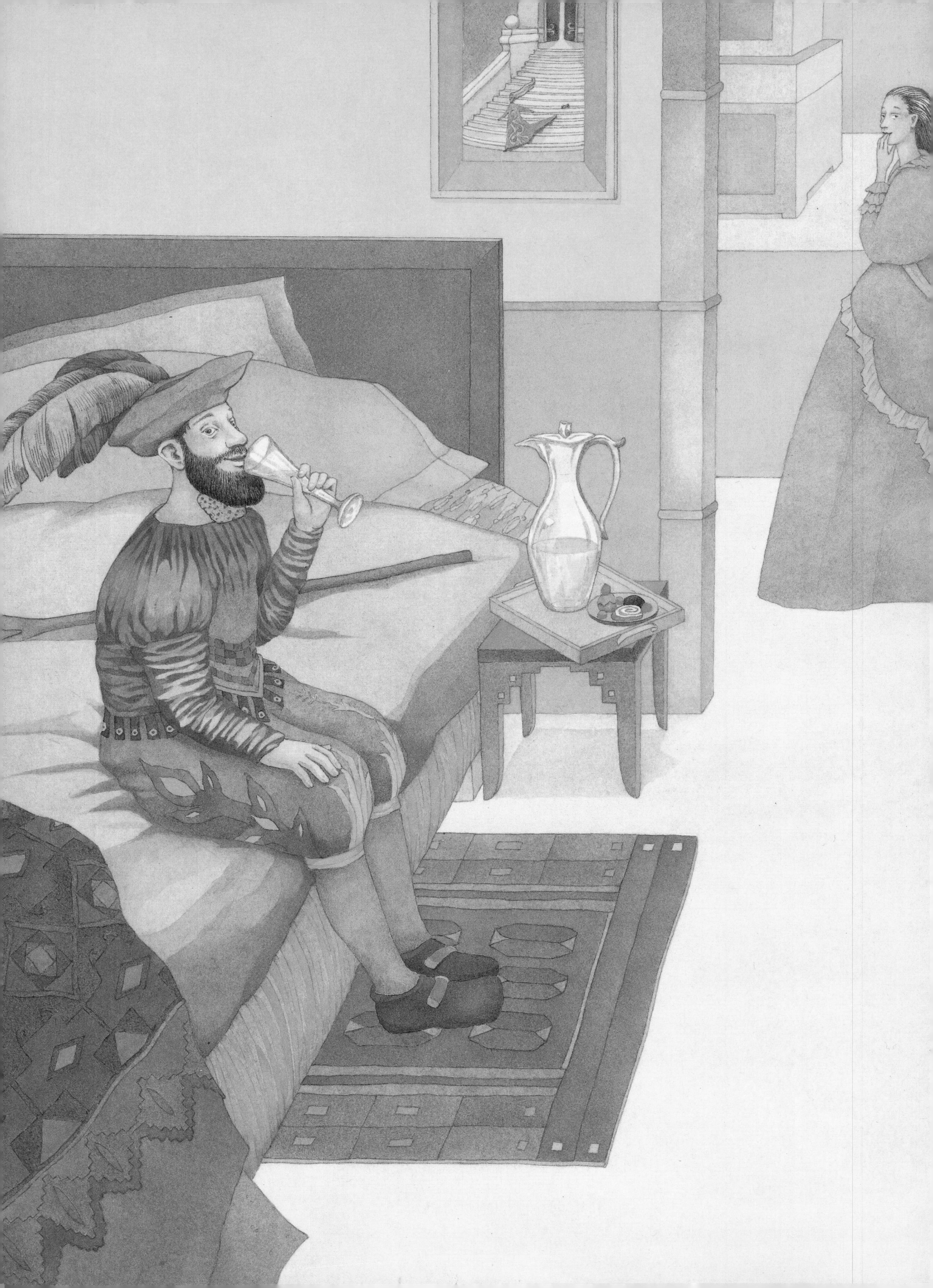

Later that evening he was taken to the room next to the princesses' great bedroom, and as he was getting ready for bed, the eldest princess brought him a goblet of wine. However, the soldier had tied a sponge under his chin. He let the wine run into the sponge, and did not drink a drop of it. Then he lay down, and when he had been lying there for a while, he began to snore as if he were fast asleep. On hearing the snores, the twelve princesses laughed, and the eldest said, "There's another man who's tired of life!"

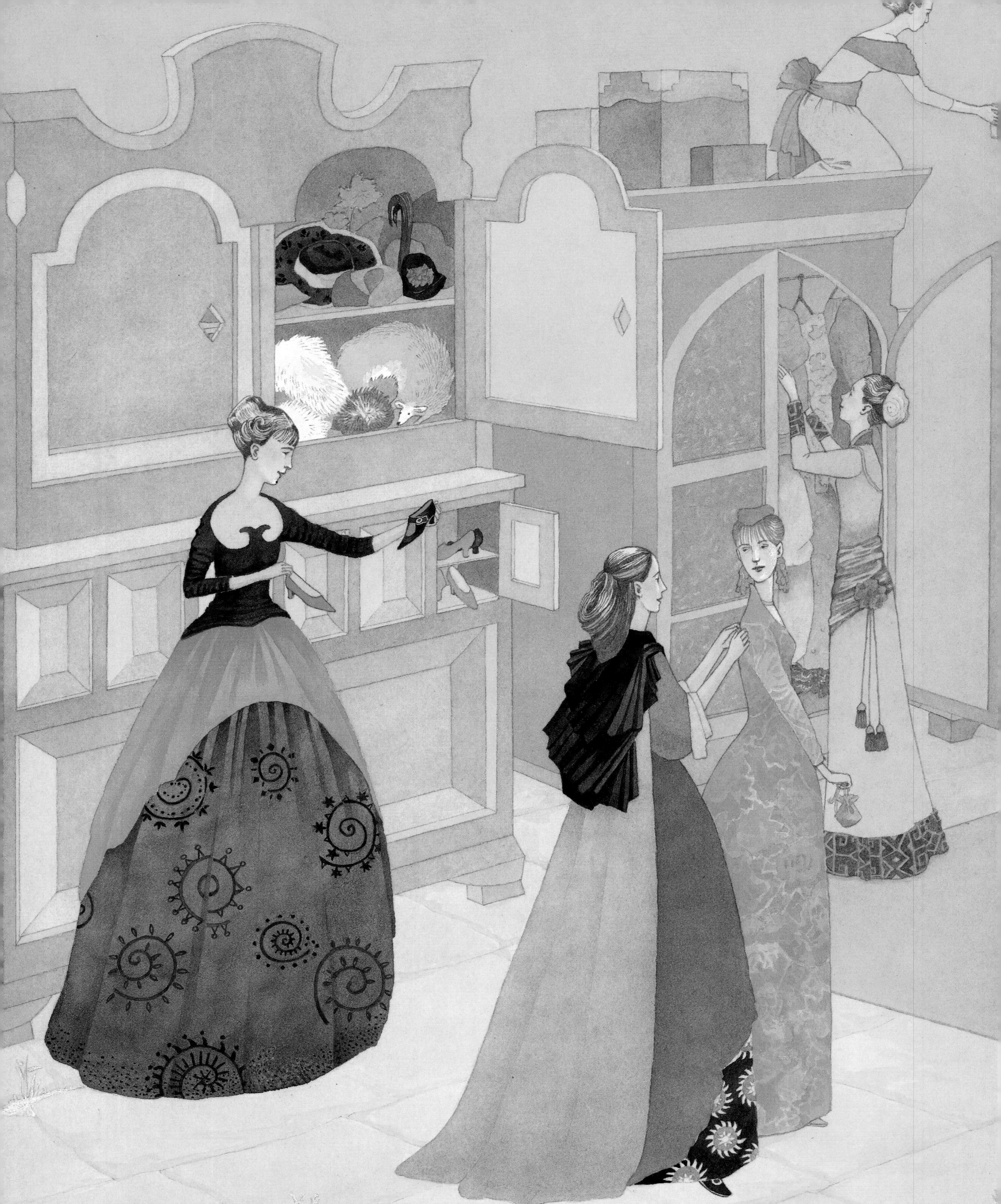

The princesses got up, opened their chests and their wardrobes, and took out magnificent gowns. They dressed in front of the mirrors, skipping about and laughing happily.

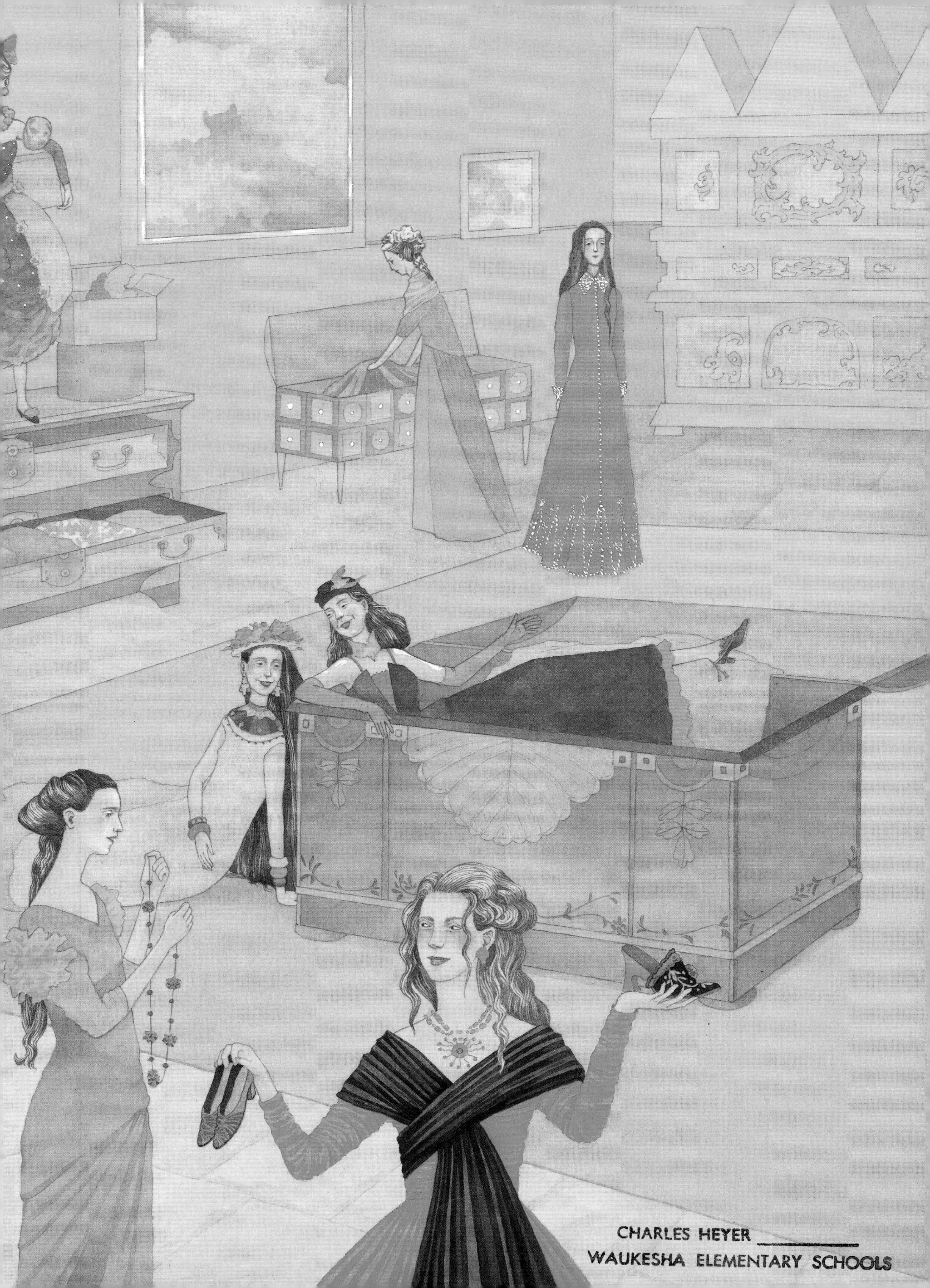

All except for the youngest princess, who said, "You're all so merry, but I feel very strange, although I don't know why. I'm sure some misfortune is going to happen."

"You're a silly goose," said the eldest princess. "You're always afraid of something. Don't you remember how many kings' sons have already tried their luck and failed?"

When they were all ready, they looked at the soldier, but he had closed his eyes and was lying perfectly still, so they felt sure he was asleep.

Then the eldest princess went over to her bed and tapped it. It immediately sank into the floor, and they climbed down through the opening one by one, led by the eldest.

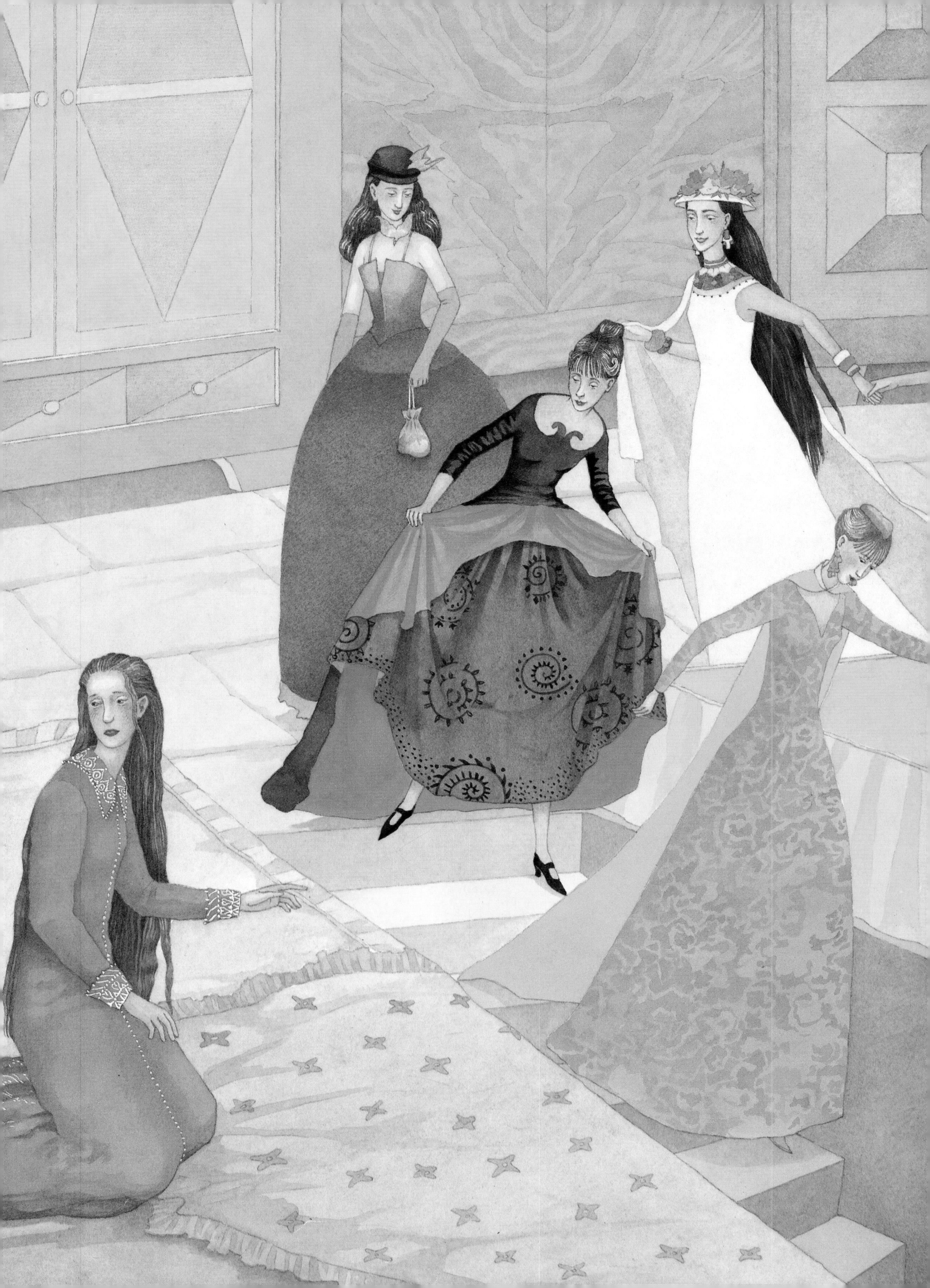

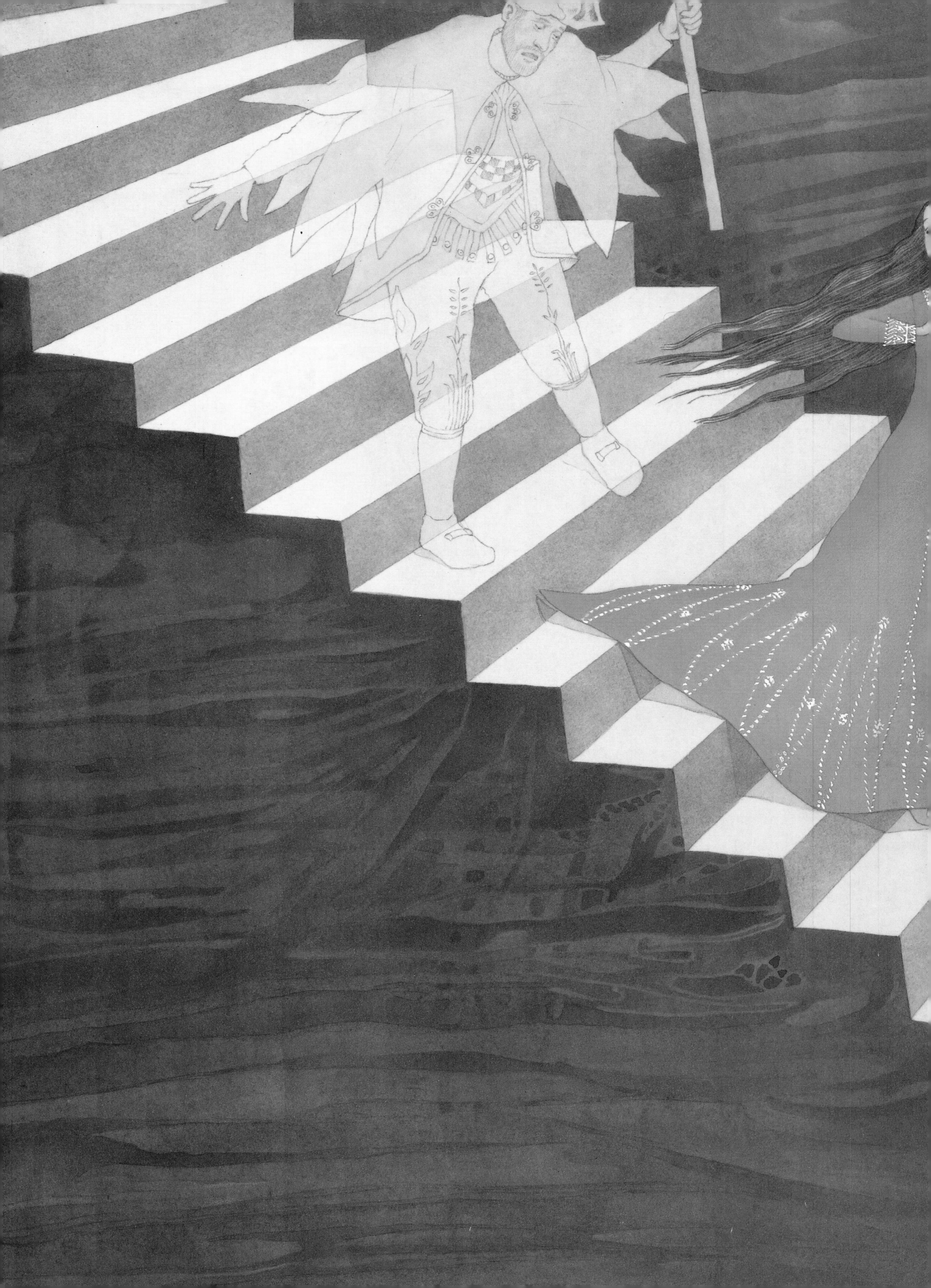

The soldier, who had seen all this, wasted no time in putting on his cape and following the youngest princess. Halfway down the stairs, he trod on the hem of her dress. She started in surprise and cried, "What was that? Who's holding my dress?"

"Don't be so silly," said the eldest princess. "You must have caught it on a nail."

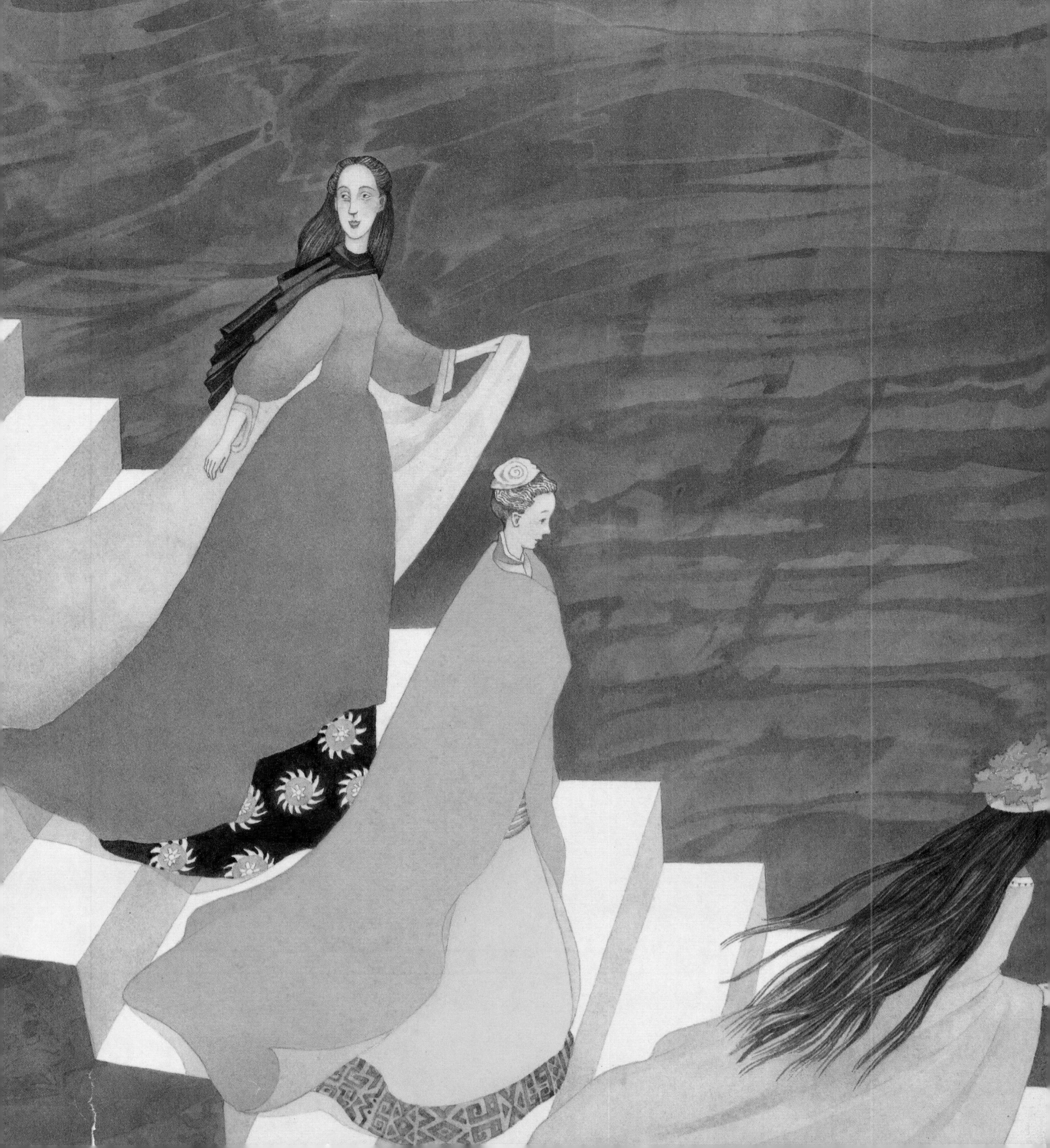

They went all the way down the stairs, and at the bottom there was a wonderful avenue of trees with leaves made of shiny, glittering silver.

The soldier thought, "I'd better take something back as proof," and he broke off a twig from one of the trees. The tree gave a great crack, and the youngest princess cried out again, "There's something wrong! Did you hear that crack?"

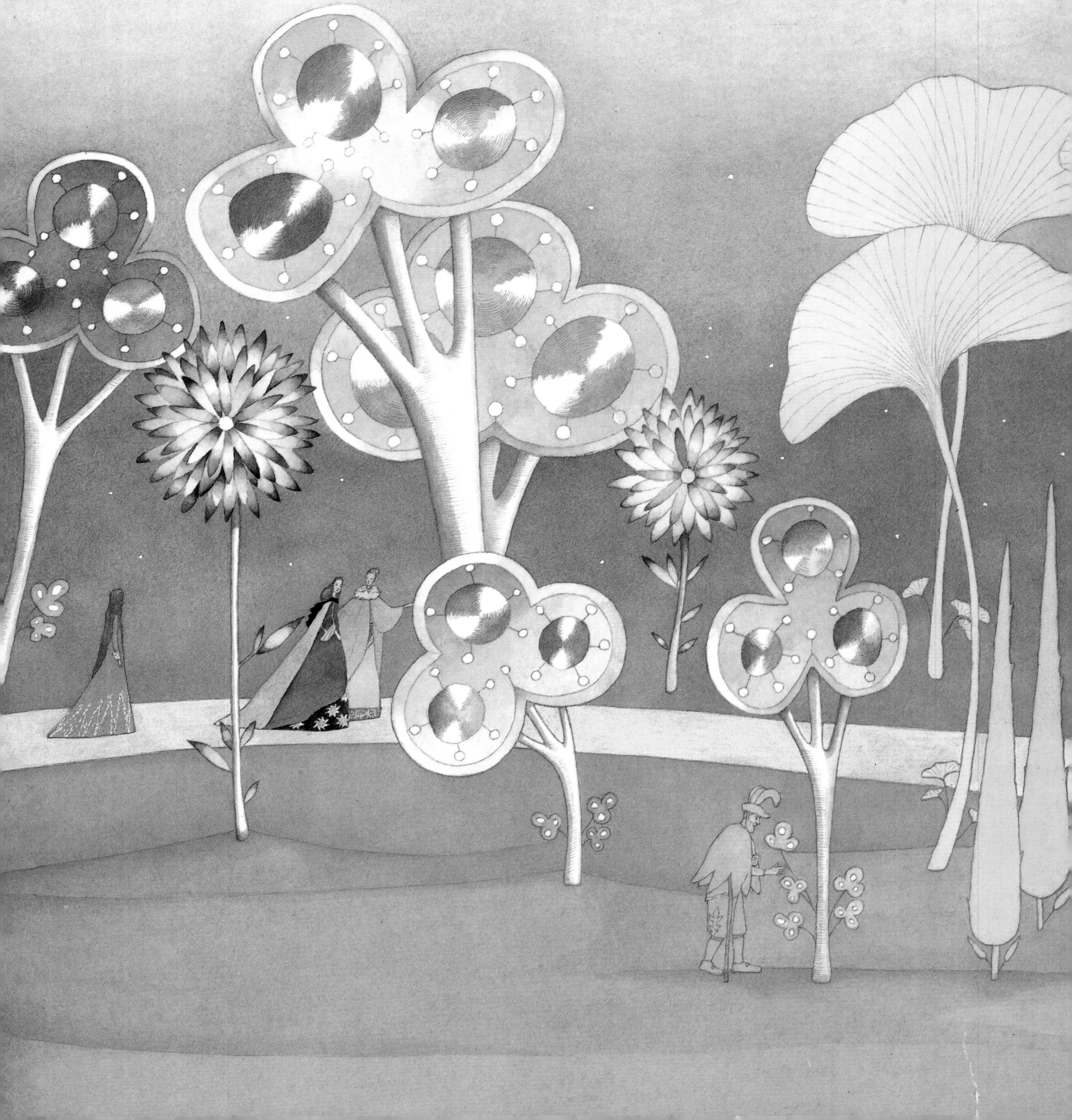

But the eldest princess said, "It's our princes, firing shots of joy to salute us, because we'll soon have set them free from the spell."

Next they came to an avenue of trees with golden leaves, and finally to a third avenue of trees with leaves made of bright diamonds. The soldier broke off a twig of gold and one of diamonds, and each time there was a crack that frightened the youngest princess, but the eldest insisted that the sounds were a salute being fired to welcome them.

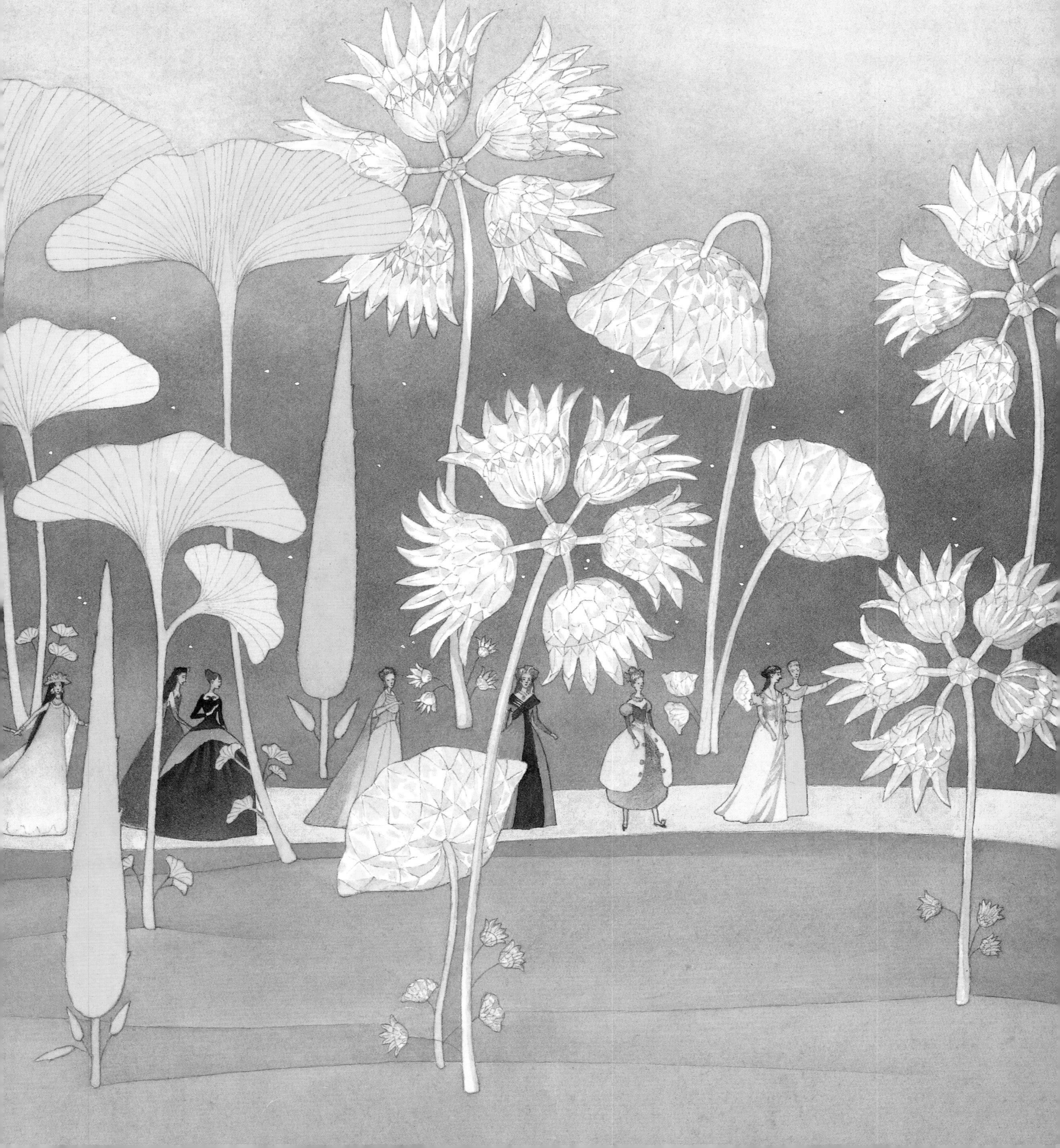

They went on, and came to a great lake with twelve little boats bobbing on the water, and a handsome prince in every boat. The princes had been waiting for the twelve princesses, and each took one of them into his boat. The soldier got into the same boat as the youngest sister. "I don't know how it is," said her prince, "but the boat seems much heavier today. I have to paddle with all my strength to make it move at all."

"It must be the warm weather," said the youngest princess. "I feel the heat myself."

On the other side of the lake stood a beautiful, brightly lit castle, filled with the merry music of drums and trumpets.

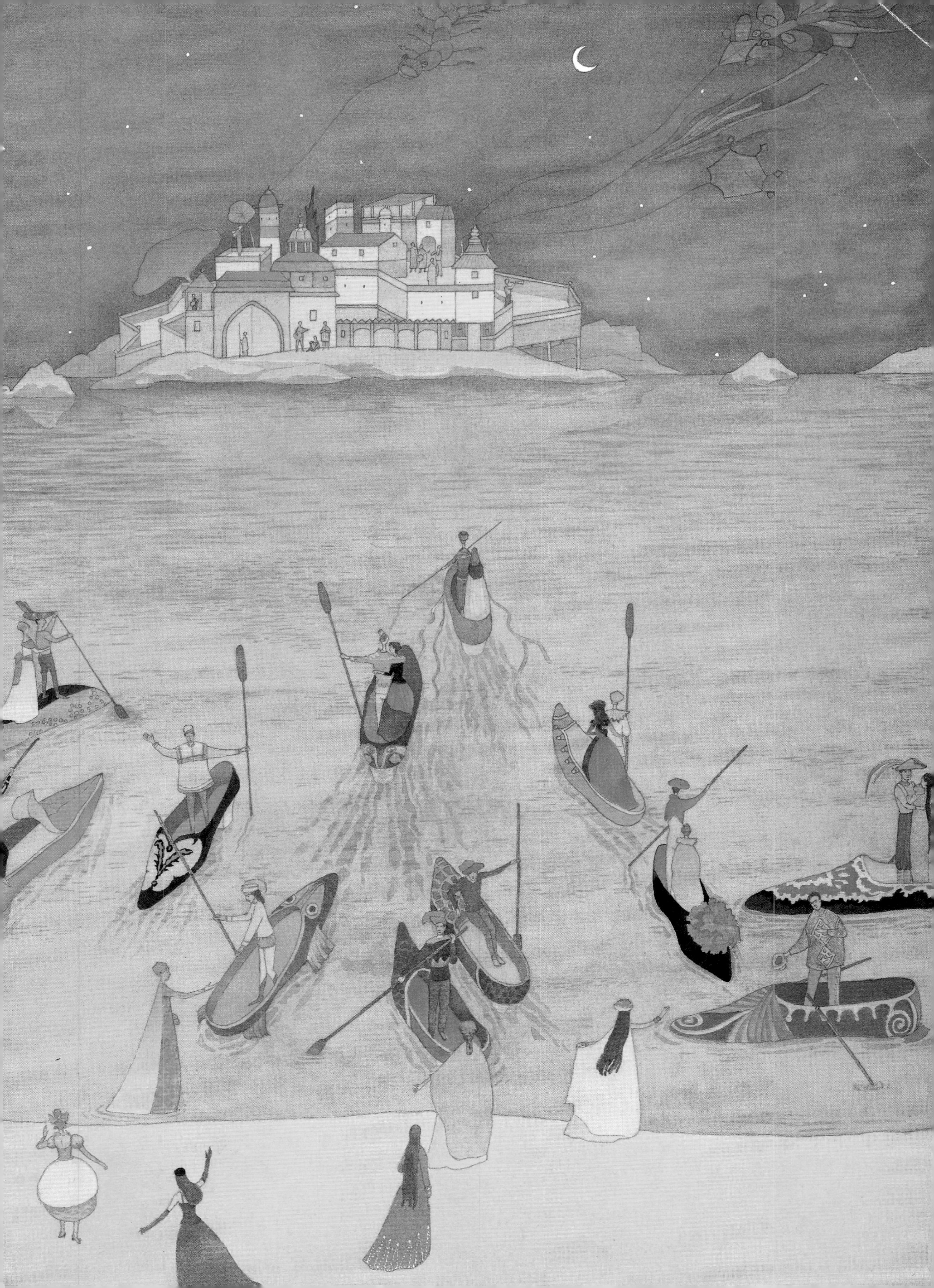

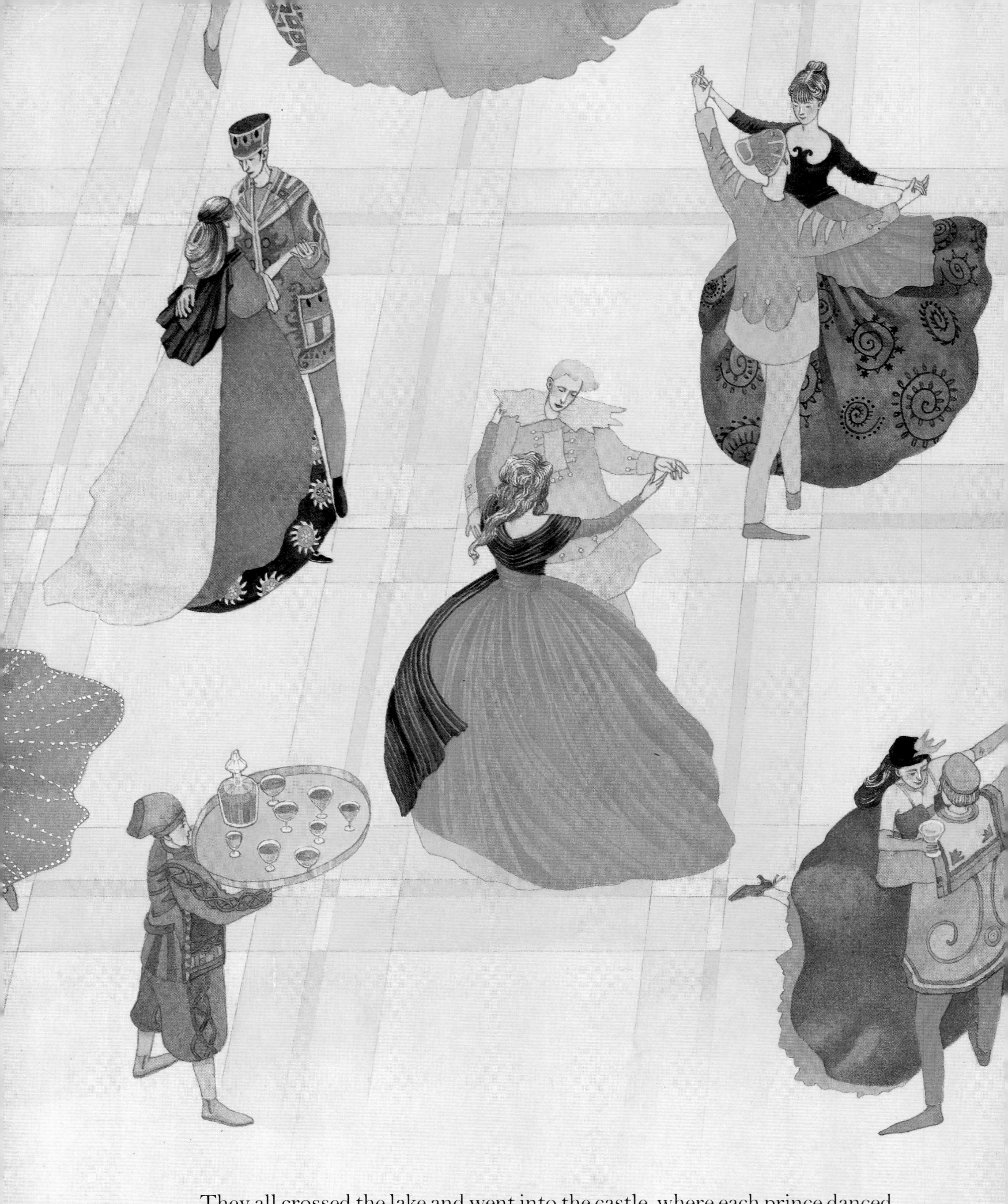

They all crossed the lake and went into the castle, where each prince danced with his sweetheart. The invisible soldier danced with them too, and when one of the princesses had a goblet of wine in her hand, he would take it and drink the wine as she was raising it to her mouth. The youngest princess was frightened, but her eldest sister kept telling her not to worry.

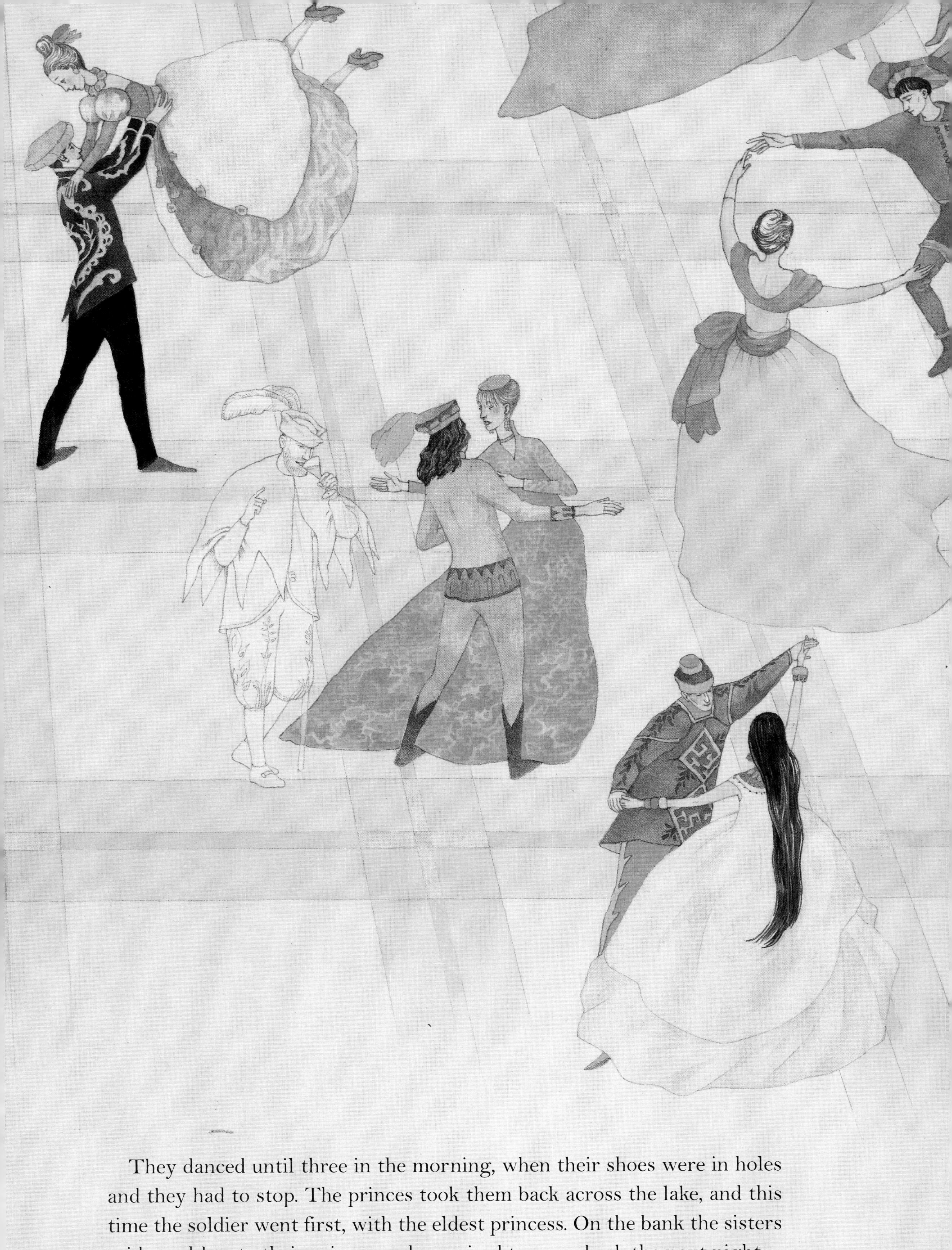

They danced until three in the morning, when their shoes were in holes and they had to stop. The princes took them back across the lake, and this time the soldier went first, with the eldest princess. On the bank the sisters said good-bye to their princes and promised to come back the next night.

When they reached the stairs, the soldier ran on ahead, removed his cape, and lay down in bed. By the time the twelve princesses came climbing slowly and wearily upstairs, he was snoring so noisily that they could all hear him. "We're safe enough from him!" they said.

They took off their beautiful gowns, put them away, placed the shoes they had danced into holes under their beds, and went to sleep. The soldier decided not to say anything yet. He wanted to see those strange sights again, so he went with the dancing princesses the second night, and the third night too. Everything was just the same as on the first night, and the princesses danced until their shoes were in holes. On the third night, however, the soldier brought away a goblet as further proof.

When the time came for the soldier to answer the king's question, he took along the three twigs and the goblet. Meanwhile, the twelve princesses stood behind the door, listening to hear what he would say.

"Well, where have my twelve daughters been to wear holes in their shoes every night?" asked the king.

"Dancing with twelve princes in a castle underground," replied the soldier. Then he told the king all he had seen and showed his proofs. So the king summoned his daughters and asked them if the soldier was telling the truth, and when they realized that their secret was discovered, and denying it would not help them, they had to admit everything.

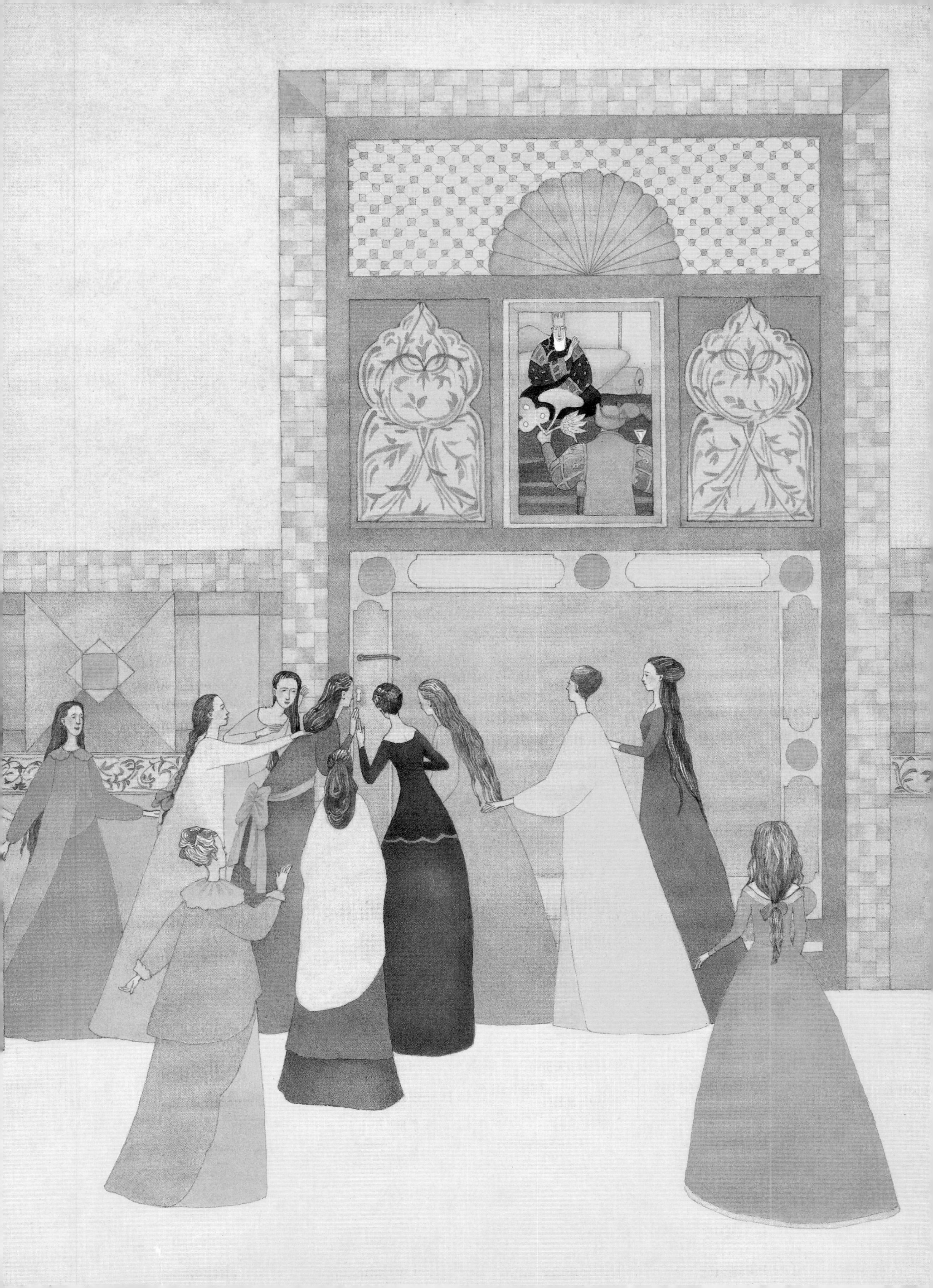

The king asked the soldier which princess he would choose for his wife, and he said, "I'm not as young as I was, so give me the eldest."

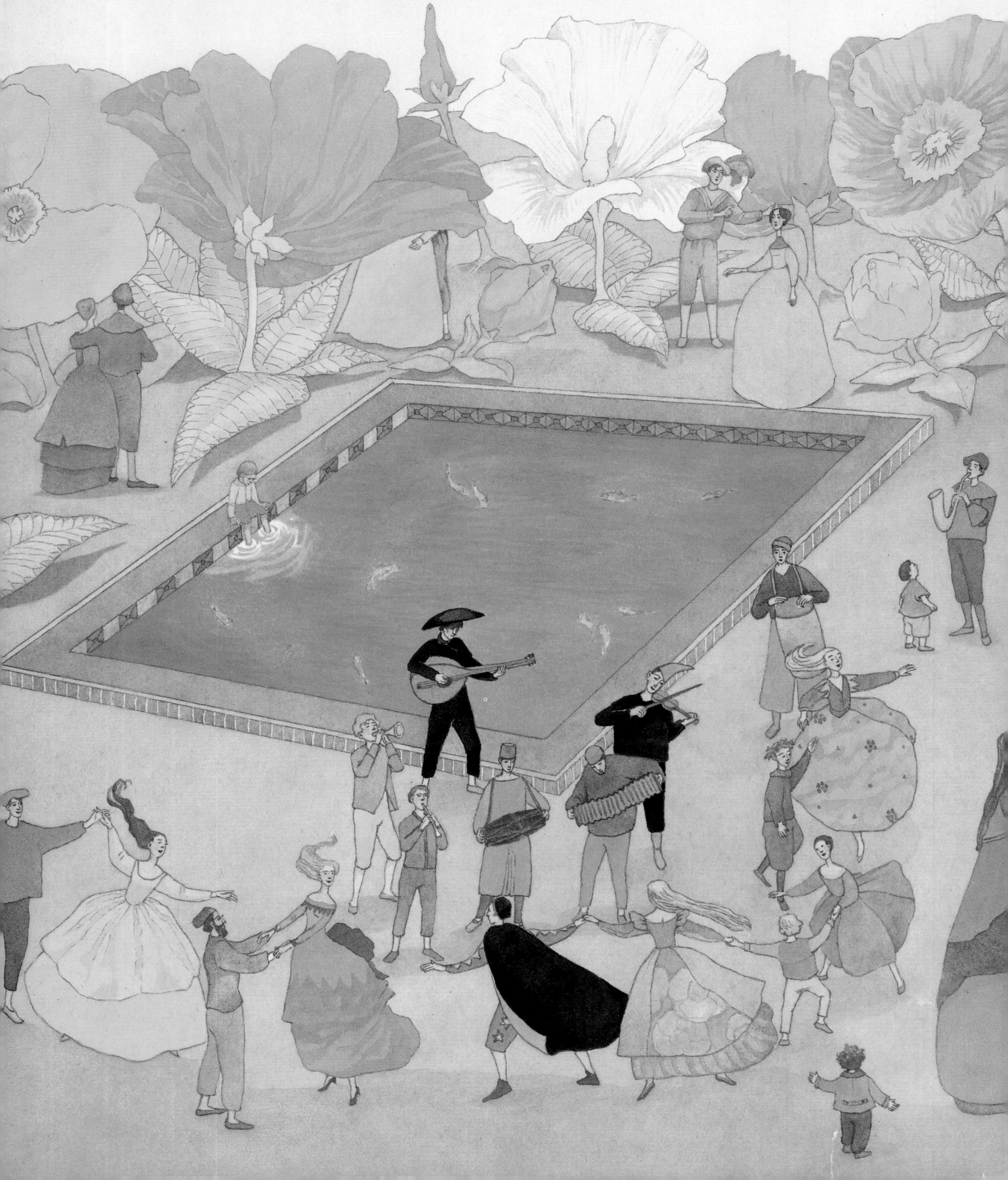

The wedding was held that very day, and the soldier was promised the crown after the old king's death.

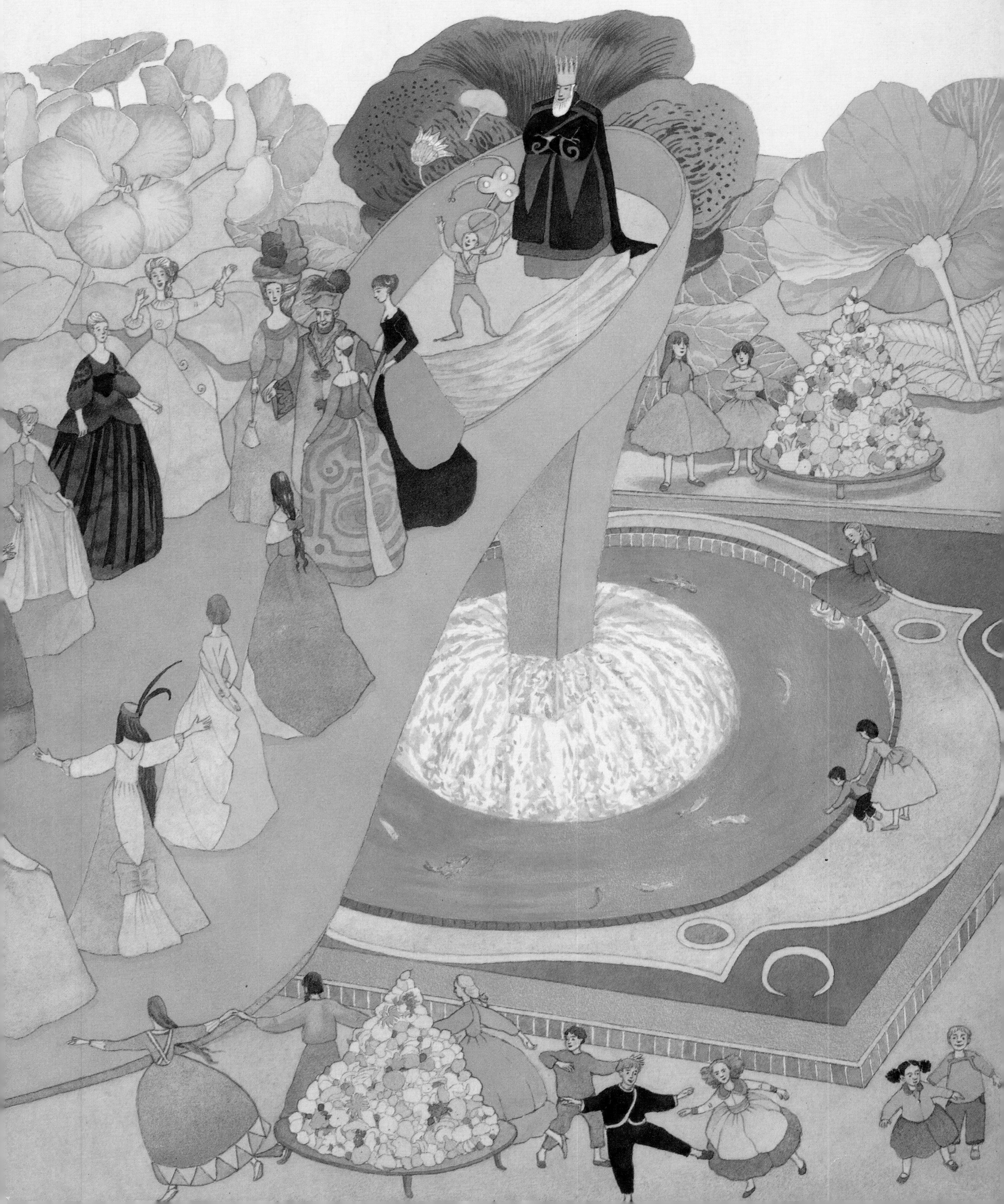

But a magic spell was cast over the princes again, and it lasted
as many days as they had spent nights dancing
with the twelve princesses.

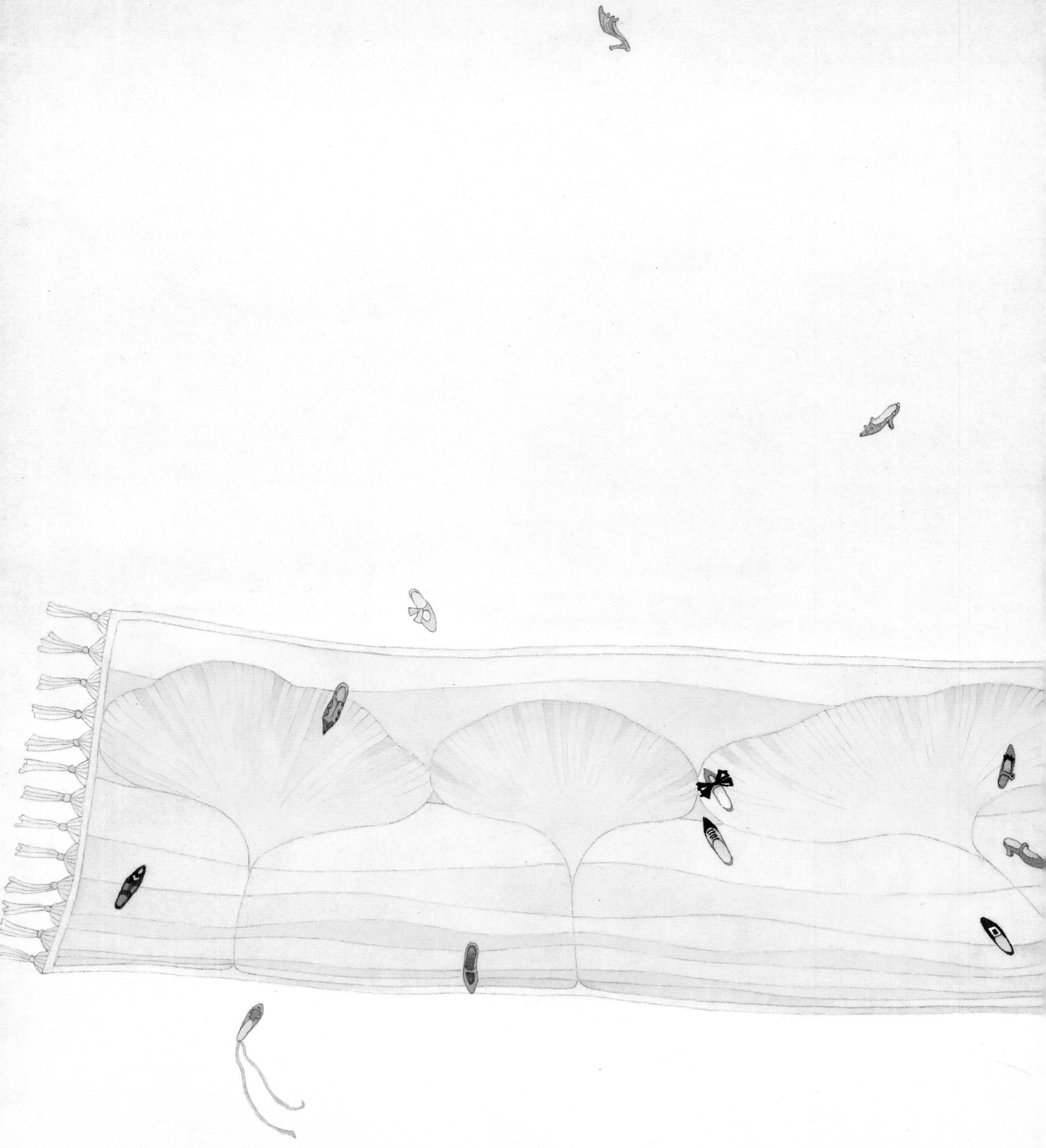

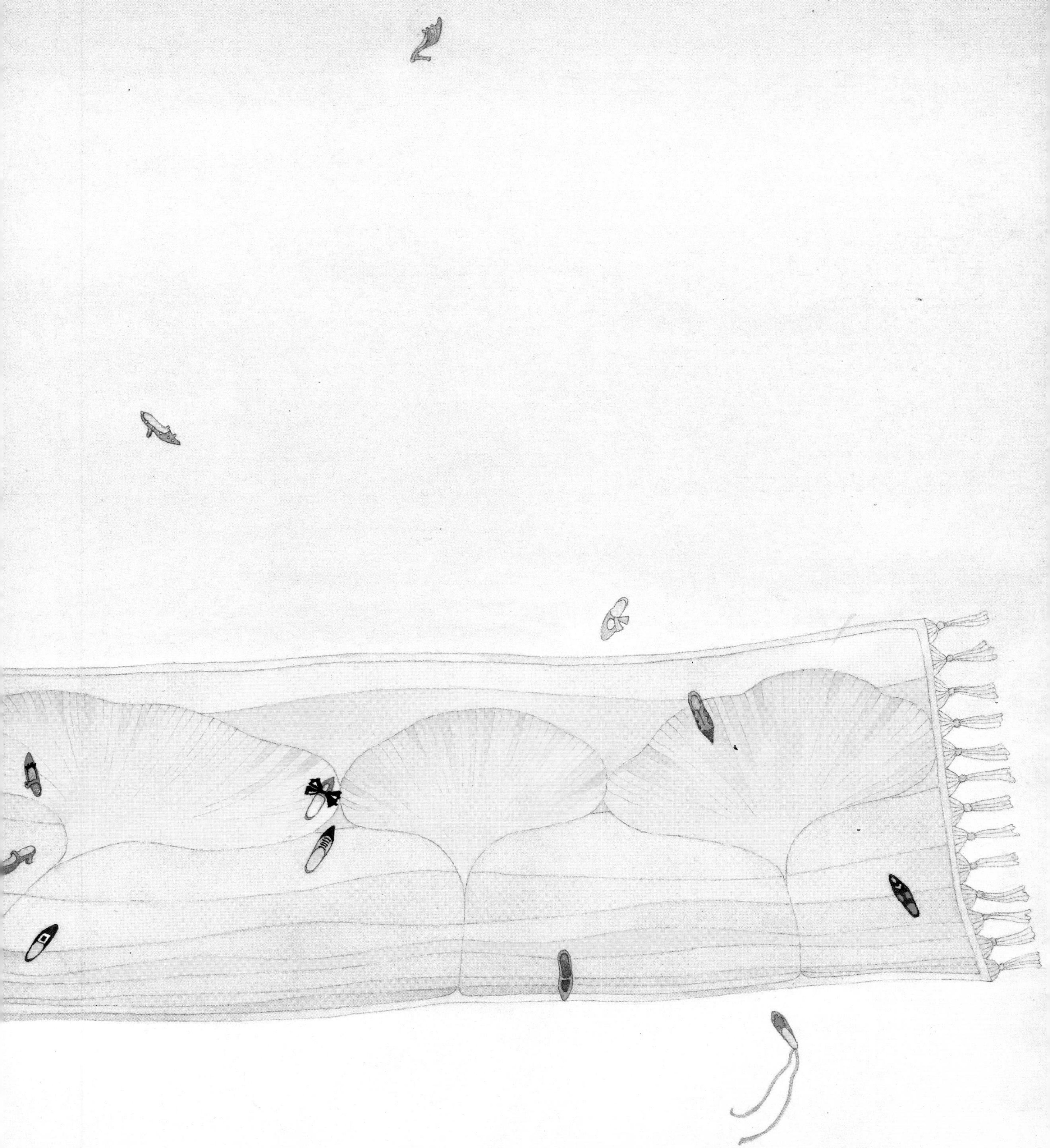

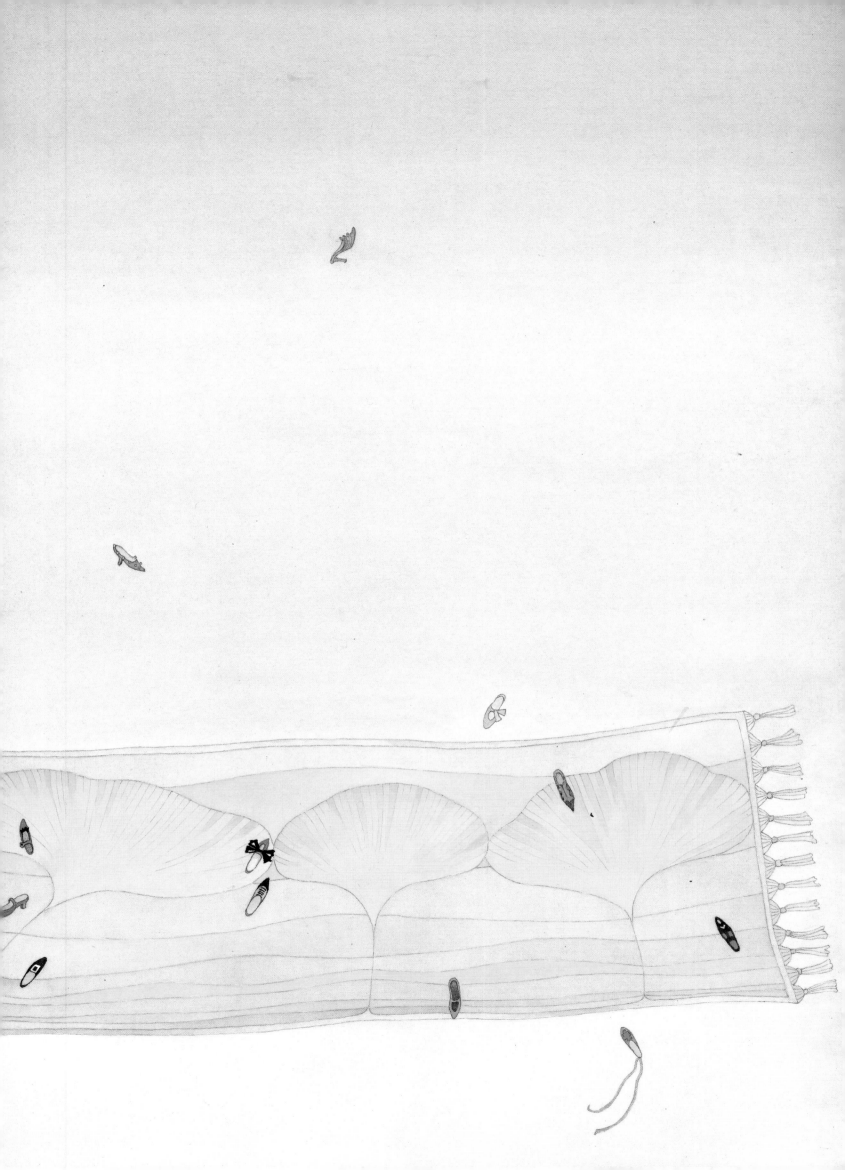